Brick by Brick

Building Our Family's Mission

Ferne Press

Written by Paul LaBaere and Illustrated by Shelley Johannes

Brick by Brick: Building Our Family's Mission
Copyright © 2014 by Paul LaBaere
Layout and cover design by Jacqueline L. Challiss Hill
Illustrations created by Shelley Johannes
Illustrations created with pencil and digital color

Printed in Canada

Summary: James and Roberto, new stepbrothers, move into their new home and find that living together can be fun but challenging at times.

Library of Congress Cataloging-in-Publication Data
LaBaere, Paul
Brick by Brick: Building Our Family's Mission/Paul LaBaere–First Edition
ISBN-13: 978-1-938326-31-8
1. Stepbrothers. 2. Blended families. 3. Family mission. 4. Unity. 5. Communication. 6. Discipline.
7. Responsibility.
I. LaBaere, Paul II. Title
Library of Congress Control Number: 2014933734

FERNE PRESS

Ferne Press is an imprint of Nelson Publishing & Marketing
366 Welch Road, Northville, MI 48167
www.nelsonpublishingandmarketing.com
(248) 735-0418

~ Dedication ~

This short story is dedicated to my three children, Paul II, Erica, and Annalise, my three stepchildren, Jackson, Ella, and Kathryn, and my beautiful wife, Beth.

I am the luckiest man and so blessed to have met Beth, who is the love of my life and my best friend.

I would like to give a special thank-you to my first cousin, Joseph Stark, for inspiring me to write this story and share it with others.

I would like to thank all of the police and firemen for their public service and dedication to the communities they serve.

Thank you, Marian Nelson, Kris Yankee, and Kathy Dyer. Marian, you gave me a chance to write my story and believed in me. Kris, thank you for guiding me through this process and for giving me your expert advice. Kathy, thank you for your encouragement from the very beginning by telling me, "You need to write this book!"

To Shelley Johannes, your art talent is God-given, and thank you for giving meaning to the words and making my story come alive.

Thank you to my parents, Richard LaBaere and MaryJoe Burns, for encouraging education and promoting college in my life. You raised me by instilling in me strong family bonds, discipline, a hard work ethic, and a lot of love. I love you both.

"How cool! Our brand-new house and we get to choose our room," James told Roberto. "Since I'm older, I get first pick!"

Roberto said, "That's not fair. My mom said I can have any room I want!"

"Too bad, Roberto. Don't be a baby!"
"You're not my boss!" Roberto yelled. "MOM!"

"I can't believe they're already bickering," John said to Maria. "Boys, the rooms are the same size. Let's not have any arguing or name calling, or there will be consequences. I think you two need to shake hands or hug."

James stuck out his hand, and Roberto lifted his arms for a hug. Both giggled and shook hands. James said, "I'm sorry. You can have first pick. I'm glad we're stepbrothers."

Later, two neighborhood kids came over to play.
"I'm Ryan and this is Becca. Is it true your dad's a policeman?
I heard policemen are mean and very strict."

"Yes, he's a policeman," James replied.
"But he's really nice and always fair.
He helps people solve their problems.
That's what policemen do.
Do you guys want to play?"

Ryan and Becca said, "For sure!"

A few weeks passed and Dad said,
"We have a surprise for you.
Go into the garage and check it out!"

James said, "Oh, yeah! New bikes!"

"How awesome! This is the best!
We love them!" exclaimed Roberto.

"Two rules, boys:
stay within sight of our house and
always wear your helmets," Dad said.

James replied, "We promise!"

The boys thanked their parents, put
on their helmets, and off they rode.

"Wanna go on a long bike ride and check out some trails?" James asked.

"Sure," said Roberto.

"Follow me. This one has lots of hills!"

James led the way, turning left, then right, then left, and then right.

After a while James said, "I'm not sure where
we are. I think we're kind of lost."

"Let's keep going.
We must be close," said Roberto.
"I wish I were home and never followed you."

Suddenly, James noticed a policeman driving by and yelled,
"We're lost. Can you help us?"

"Sure thing," said the officer. "Hey, I work with your dad."
He loaded up the bikes and drove the boys home.

Mom and Dad were in the driveway.
Mom said, "You really had us worried.
Lucky Dad made some calls and
one of his officers found you."

"Park the bikes.
You can't ride them for a week," said Dad.
"Head straight to your rooms. You broke your
promises and there are consequences."

In his bedroom, James said to himself,
"Why didn't I just listen?"

Dad came in and said, "Rules are made for
reasons, and you didn't follow them.
I hope you learned your lesson.
I love you too much
to see something bad happen."

James looked into his dad's eyes and said,
"I'm sorry. I love you, too."

"Summer's finally here!" said James.
"We can play outside all day if we want.
This will be the best summer of our lives."

"I see Ryan and Becca coming over to play.
Race you to the slide!"

"You can't beat me. I'm older and I'm first!"

The two began pushing each other
and Roberto fell to the ground.
James sprinted to the slide and
touched it way before Roberto.

"You always have to be first!" said Roberto.

"You shoved me and I scraped my knee!" pouted Roberto.

Becca said, "That's not nice what you did, James. Now he's hurt."

"He's just being a little brat and always wanting attention," replied James.

Ryan said, "That was mean.
Here come your mom and dad."

In a stern voice, Dad said, "That's enough! There's no fighting in our family. Meet me by the pile of bricks. I've got a little job for both of you."

"This is the third time you've made poor choices,
so you'll move the brick pile together from
the back of the house
to the end of our property.
The bricks will be stacked evenly
and neatly until it's done."

"Aww...that's gonna take forever,"
said James.

"Now, hit the bricks!"

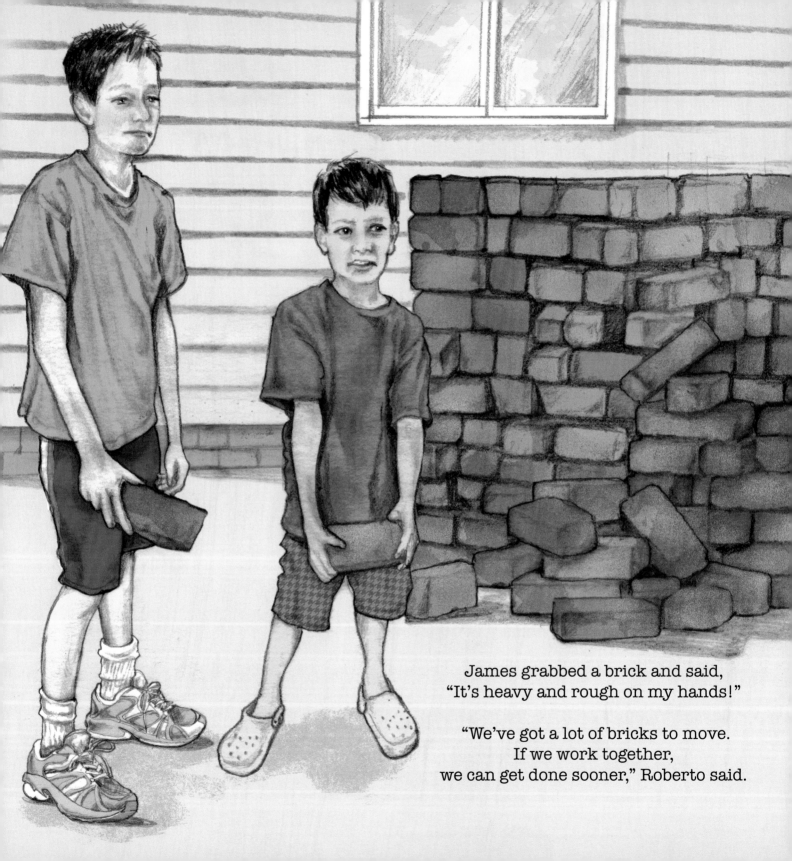

James grabbed a brick and said,
"It's heavy and rough on my hands!"

"We've got a lot of bricks to move.
If we work together,
we can get done sooner," Roberto said.

After stacking all the bricks, James said,
"I never want to hit the bricks again.
From now on, I'll try to be a better stepbrother
and never get us into trouble again. I'm sorry."

"That sounds great, and I agree on never moving those bricks again."

"Now let's go tell Mom and Dad we're done," James replied.

"We want to have a strong and happy family.
Let's talk about what's important.
How can we do that?" asked Mom.

James said, "Let's make a list.
I think we should make good choices."

Roberto added, "We should work together!"

"Always be kind to each other," Mom stated.

Dad added,
"I think it's important to respect
one another and each other's feelings.
That's called empathy."

"These are great ideas," Dad said. "I have one more. Be responsible for your own actions. Are you all ready to do your part now?"

"If we agree, let's all sign it," Mom suggested.

As James hung it on the
refrigerator, he said,
"I will always remember
what's important to me...
all of you. Come on,
Roberto, let's go outside.
Race you to the slide!"

"Not again," said Roberto.

James said, "This time you're first
because I'm the older brother who
should set a good example."

"Thanks, James. That's awesome!"

Dear Readers,

I was inspired to write this book after hearing a story told by my first cousin, Joseph Stark. He loved his sons immensely but also believed in consequences for making bad decisions. Joe would have his sons move a stack of bricks from the back of the house to the end of the property line. Joe would watch his sons working together, carrying brick after brick until they were stacked neatly and evenly. He told me his sons didn't really like moving the bricks, but they learned a lot while doing it and learned to love and respect each other. His sons became good men and often thanked their dad for his love and discipline and for giving them the guidance to be successful in life.

I believe it is important in life to learn from our parents, who guide and support us along the way. Being a parent is not an easy task and it is never-ending. I have always asked my parents for advice and help, and their love and guidance continue throughout my adulthood.

I hope that after reading my book young children and siblings realize the importance of family, love, and consequences. I hope this book encourages children to make good choices and always treat family members with kindness and love.

Paul LaBaere

~ How to Create a Family Mission ~

Here are some guidelines for creating your own family mission:

1. Talk to your family about developing a family mission.
2. Sit down, as a family, and come up with ideas of how your family should treat each other.
3. Be sure to get input from all members and then write out their statements.
4. Keep it positive and healthy for all.
5. Try to include words like respect, kindness, empathy, trust, support, and working together.
6. When everyone agrees with the wording, have each person sign the mission.
7. Post your Family Mission in a location where all can see it.
8. Remind each person that they are responsible for their own behavior (no blaming).
9. Refer to it often as a guideline for good family communication.

LaBaere Family Mission

Every day we love each other for who we are and who we will be. We respect each other and all of our feelings to make our house a happy home. We will build strong bonds of trust through honesty and good communication. Each person is responsible for his or her own actions and behaviors. Strive to do your best in everything you do and make each day better than the last for all.

Paul LaBaere was raised by his parents in Mount Clemens, Michigan, along with his two sisters and one brother. Throughout his life he developed a strong work ethic by working with his family on their grandparents' farm. He earned a bachelor's degree in Criminal Justice from Michigan State University. He has attended numerous courses in Advanced Police Education.

Paul has been a police officer for the Sterling Heights Police Department for more than twenty-five years and has achieved the rank of sergeant. Paul is a highly decorated veteran officer who has received numerous awards. He has also been an instructor for over thirteen years at Macomb Community College Police Academy for pursuit driving.

Paul loves the outdoors and is an avid sportsman. He stresses education to all his children, nieces, and nephews. Paul loves his family, enjoys his job, and has dreamed of writing a children's book for several years. For more information about Paul, please visit www.paullabaerebooks.com.

Shelley Johannes began her artistic career after ten years in the architectural design industry. While that was fun, she found her dream job when motherhood introduced her to the world of children's books. Five years and a dozen books later, she still pinches herself every day. A library fanatic who used to walk to the bus stop with her nose in a book, Shelley still reads every chance she gets. Iced cappuccinos and book recommendations are her favorite gifts. Shelley wishes she could live in perpetual autumn, but for now she lives in Michigan where she enjoys the colorful chaos of life with her husband, Bob, and their two boys, Matthew and Nolan. When she's not painting or playing with her boys, she writes about her adventures in books at thebookdiariesblog.com.